curvy girl for the boss

emma bray

one

. . .

Chrissy

I STAND BEFORE THE MIRROR, studying my reflection as I slip into the elegant white dress, the fabric shimmering under the warm glow of my bedroom lights. The bodice hugs my curves, the off-the-shoulder neckline exposing the creamy skin of my décolletage. I let out a soft exhale, my fingers trembling slightly as I smooth the skirt over my hips.

"You look stunning, Chrissy," my best friend Madison says from behind me, her voice laced with admiration. "That dress is perfect for Christine Daaé."

I meet her eyes in the mirror, a smile playing at the corners of my lips. "Thanks, Mads. I can't believe I'm actually doing this—going to a fancy costume party the night before starting my dream job."

Madison grins, stepping closer to adjust the delicate lace trim along the neckline of my dress. "You deserve to celebrate! Landing that marketing position at Zander Industries is huge. Besides, it's Halloween!"

I nod and grin, a flutter of excitement and nerves dancing in my stomach at the mention of my new job. Of course, Madison would say that. She's always looking for any excuse to drag me to a party. She's definitely the fun-loving one between us two best friends.

"I just hope I can live up to everyone's expectations. Zander Williams is known for being a brilliant but demanding boss," I say as I bite my lip, my nervousness taking back over.

"You've got this, girl! You're smart, talented, and you look hot as hell in that costume. Stop worrying about tomorrow! Tonight is all about letting loose and enjoying yourself before diving into the corporate world."

I take a deep breath, letting her words sink in as I turn back to my reflection. The dress fits like a second skin, the layered skirt cascading down my legs in a whisper of satin and lace. I reach for the delicate white mask resting on my vanity, my fingers caressing the smooth porcelain surface before lifting it to my face.

As I secure the mask in place, a thrill rushes through me, the nerves giving way to anticipation. I may be starting a new chapter in my life tomorrow, but tonight, I'm going to embrace the mystery and magic of being someone else entirely—even if only for a few hours.

"All right, let's do this," I say as I turn to face Madison with a grin.

***

The moment I step into the ballroom, I'm transported to another world. The space is transformed, draped in rich fabrics and bathed in the warm glow of countless candles. Masked figures swirl around me, their costumes a dazzling array of colors and textures. It's like something from another era, and I'm momentarily dumbstruck. The air is thick with anticipation, charged with a sense of mystery and barely restrained desire.

I pause for a moment, drinking it all in. The music wraps around me like an intimate caress. I've never been to a masquerade before, and the sheer romance of it all sends a shiver down my spine.

Madison appears at my elbow, her eyes sparkling behind her own intricately decorated mask. "Isn't this incredible?" she murmurs, her voice nearly lost in the swell of the music.

I nod, too entranced to speak. As I let my gaze wander over the room, a flicker of awareness prickles along my skin, and I turn slowly, my gaze drawn like a magnet to the far side of the room. There, amid the swirling dancers and flickering candlelight, stands a figure that seems to command attention without even trying. He's dressed as the Phantom, the stark white of his half-mask contrasting sharply with the elegant black of his tailored suit.

A little thrill runs through me. How perfect! A man dressed as a character that matches mine.

Our eyes meet, and the rest of the room falls away. It's as if we're the only two people in the world, connected by an invisible thread that tugs insistently at my core. I'm vaguely aware of Madison saying something, but her words are lost in the rush of blood in my ears.

The Phantom tilts his head, a silent invitation, and I find myself moving towards him as if in a dream. The crowds part before me, the chatter and laughter fading to a distant hum. As I draw closer, I see that his eyes are a striking blue, piercing even in the dim light. They seem to see straight into my soul, leaving me feeling exposed and exhilarated all at once.

"Good evening," he says, his voice a rich, velvety purr that sends a shiver cascading down my spine. "I don't believe we've met."

"No," I manage, my own voice sounding breathy and foreign to my ears. "I'm sure I would remember."

His lips quirk in a ghost of a smile. "Likewise. And who, may I ask, is the enchanting Christine to my Phantom tonight?"

I flush, suddenly grateful for the mask that conceals my heated cheeks. "Chrissy," I murmur, extending a hand that trembles slightly. "My name is Chrissy."

He takes my hand in his, his fingers warm and strong. Instead of shaking it, he raises it to his lips, brushing a feather-light kiss across my knuckles. "A pleasure, Chrissy. You may call me...Erik."

I laugh softly, caught up in the playful spirit of the masquerade. "Just like the Phantom's real name. How fitting."

"Indeed," he agrees, his eyes glinting with mischief. "It seems we are perfectly matched this evening."

There's a double meaning to his words, a subtle

undercurrent that makes my pulse quicken. The air between us feels charged, electric with possibility. I wonder if he feels it too, this inexplicable connection.

My cheeks flush further. I've never been this intensely attracted to someone—someone I just met no less.

"So, Chrissy," he says, my name rolling off his tongue like a caress. "What brings a stunning creature like you to this den of mystery and intrigue tonight? Business or pleasure?"

I smile, emboldened by the mask and the magic of the moment. "Can't it be both? I do start a new job tomorrow, so I suppose this is my last hurrah, so to speak. A final night of freedom before the corporate world claims me."

He chuckles, the sound rich and warm. "Ah, so we have a woman of ambition in our midst. I admire that. And your new employer is fortunate indeed to have secured your talents."

I laugh, shaking my head. "You're very smooth, Erik. But I think it's a bit early to be singing my praises. For all you know, I could be utterly incompetent."

"Nonsense," he scoffs, his gaze intense. "I have a feeling about you, Chrissy. Call it...intuition. I suspect you're going to take the corporate world by storm."

A haunting melody drifts through the air, the notes slow and seductive. The Phantom offers me his hand, his eyes gleaming behind his mask. "Dance with me," he murmurs, and it's not a question.

I place my hand in his, letting him draw me close. His other hand settles at the small of my back, the heat of his touch searing through the thin fabric of my dress. We begin to move, our bodies swaying in perfect synchronicity, as if we've been dancing together for years.

The world around us fades away, until there is only the music, the dance, and this man who has so thoroughly captivated me. I'm acutely aware of every place our bodies touch—the brush of his thigh against mine, the firmness of his chest pressed to my breasts, the whisper of his breath against my cheek.

As the song builds to a crescendo, Zander spins me out, then pulls me back in, my back now pressed firmly to his front. His lips graze the shell of my ear as he whispers, "You move like a dream, Chrissy. Like you were made to be in my arms."

I shiver, my body alight with sensation. I turn in his embrace, our faces now mere inches apart.

"Maybe I was," I breathe, hardly recognizing my own voice, husky with desire.

His gaze drops to my lips, and I see the hunger in his eyes, a mirror of my own. "I want to kiss you," he says, his grip on my waist tightening. "I want to do a lot more than kiss you."

My breath catches, and my mind races. I never do anything impulsive. I'm always the responsible straight-laced one. Isn't tonight supposed to be about celebrating and finally letting lose?

His eyes smolder down at me, and I lick my lips. Fuck it. "Then what are you waiting for?" I finally whisper, throwing caution to the wind.

He emits a growl in the back of his throat, and then his mouth claims mine in a searing kiss, and holy moly, I'm lost. Lost in the feel of his lips moving over mine, in the slide of his tongue against my own, in the way his hands roam over my curves, leaving trails of fire in their wake.

We stumble off the dance floor, never breaking the kiss, until we find ourselves in a dimly lit corner, hidden from prying eyes. He presses me against the wall, his body a delicious weight against mine. "God, Chrissy," he groans as he kisses a path down my neck. "What is this madness? I can't get enough of you. I've never wanted anyone the way I want you."

"Same," I gasp, my fingers tangling in his hair, holding him to me.

He presses himself against, and I can feel his erection poking into my stomach.

My eyes widen. He's fucking huge! I might be a virgin, but I've read books before and sneaked a peak at some porn, and I know he's more than well endowed.

He growls again and takes my hand before leading me down a hallway and into a room that looks like an old-world library or study.

His hands find the zipper of my dress, lowering it slowly, torturously. "Let me worship you," he murmurs against my skin. "Let me show you pleasure like you've never known."

I nod, unable to form words, my body trembling with need. He slides the dress from my shoulders, letting it pool at my feet. I stand before him in nothing but my lacy white bra and panties, feeling exposed yet utterly desired under his heated gaze.

"Exquisite," he breathes, his hands skimming over my bare skin, leaving goosebumps in their wake. "An angel in the flesh."

Damn, he's playing this Phantom role good, and I'm so here for it.

He dips his head, trailing open-mouthed kisses along my collarbone, his fingers deftly unclasping my bra. It falls away, and he cups my breasts, his thumbs brushing over my nipples, coaxing them to hardened peaks. I arch into his touch, a soft moan escaping my lips.

"So responsive," he murmurs appreciatively. "I can't wait to taste every inch of you."

He lowers me onto a plush velvet chaise, his body covering mine. His mouth finds my breast, suckling and nipping, while his hand traces the curve of my waist, my hip, before slipping between my thighs. He groans when he feels the damp heat there, evidence of my arousal.

"All this for me?" he asks, his fingers stroking me through the fabric of my panties.

"Yes," I hiss, my hips lifting to meet his touch. "Please, Erik...I need..."

"Shh, I know what you need, sweet Chrissy. Let me give it to you."

He strips away my panties and settles between my legs, his breath hot against my most intimate flesh. The first stroke of his tongue has me crying out, my hands fisting in his hair. He licks and suckles, worshipping me with his mouth, driving me to heights I've never known.

When he slips a finger inside me, I nearly come undone. "Please," I beg, not even sure what I'm pleading for.

He adds a second finger, stretching me, preparing me. "I want to be inside you," he rasps. "I want to claim you, make you mine."

"Yes," I breathe. "Yes, please."

He stands, shedding his clothes with impressive speed. And then he's back, the hard heat of him pressing against my entrance. He pauses, his eyes locking with mine. "You're sure?" he asks, and I can see the strain on his face, the effort it's taking to hold back.

"I've never been more sure of anything," I tell him, and it's the truth.

He surges forward, filling me in one swift thrust. I cry out at the sudden fullness, the slight pinch of pain. He stills, his eyes widening as realization dawns on him. "You're a virgin?"

I flush and bite my lip as I nod.

He makes a sound that's half tortured, half pleasure as he stays still, letting me adjust, and then he does something that causes takes my breath away with its sudden tenderness.

He peppers my face with gentle kisses. "Breathe, baby," he soothes. "Just breathe."

I do, focusing on the feel of him inside me, the

He begins to move, slowly at first, his strokes deep and measured. Each thrust sends a wave of pleasure radiating through my body, and soon the discomfort fades, replaced by a building ecstasy. I wrap my legs around his waist, urging him deeper, and he groans, his control slipping.

"God, Chrissy," he pants against my neck. "You feel incredible. So tight, so perfect."

His words inflame me further, and I arch against him, meeting him thrust for thrust. The room fills with the sounds of our passion—the slap of skin on skin, our mingled moans and gasps, the erotic whisper of the velvet beneath us.

"You're mine now," he growls, his thrusts becoming harder, more possessive. "Say it, Chrissy. Say you're mine."

A thrill runs through me at his commanding tone, at the raw need in his voice. "I'm yours," I breathe, meaning it with every fiber of my being. "All yours, Erik."

He makes a sound of pure male satisfaction and drives into me harder, hitting a spot deep inside that has me seeing stars. I rake my nails down his back, lost in the overwhelming sensations.

"I'll never let you go," he vows, his eyes burning into mine. "You belong to me now, body and soul. No other man will ever touch you. You're mine, forever and always."

His possessive words should scare me, but instead they fill me with a dark, forbidden excitement. The idea of belonging to this mysterious, powerful man is intoxicating.

"Yes," I moan, tightening my legs around him. "Yours, only yours."

He kisses me fiercely, his tongue plundering my mouth as he pounds into me, driving us both closer to the edge. I feel the tension building, coiling tighter and tighter in my belly.

"Come for me, Chrissy," he commands, his voice rough with need. "Let me feel you come undone around me."

His words are my undoing. With a cry, I shatter, my body convulsing around him as wave after wave of ecstasy crashes over me. He follows me over the edge with a roar, spilling himself deep inside me.

We cling to each other as we come down from the high, our bodies trembling, our breath coming in ragged gasps. He presses tender kisses to my face, my neck, murmuring words of praise and adoration.

"That was...incredible," I manage, my voice hoarse. "I've never felt anything like that before."

He smiles, a slow, sensual curve of his lips. "And you never will, with anyone else. You're ruined for other men now, sweet Chrissy. You'll crave my touch, my kiss, the feel of me inside you.

No one else will ever satisfy you." He growls, "No one else will ever touch you. I'll kill anyone who tries."

I shiver at his words, a thrill racing down my spine. His possessiveness, the intensity of his claim on me, it's intoxicating. A part of me knows this is crazy. But a larger part, the part that's still drunk on the pleasure he just gave me, wants to surrender completely.

"No one else," I agree breathlessly, my fingers tracing the strong line of his jaw. "I don't want anyone else. Just you."

His eyes blaze with satisfaction and something else, something deeper and more primal. He captures my hand, pressing a kiss to my palm. "Good girl," he murmurs. "My perfect, obedient angel."

He shifts, slipping out of me, and I whimper at the sudden emptiness. He chuckles, the sound dark and rich. "Don't worry, baby. We're far from done. I plan to keep you in this room until you can't walk straight. Until the only name you remember is mine."

Before I can even protest that I have to start my new job tomorrow, he's kissing me again, his mouth hot and demanding against mine. He presses me back into the plush velvet, his body covering mine, and all thoughts flee as I'm lost once more in a haze of pleasure.

He takes me again and again, until the candles burn low and the music from the ballroom fades to a distant hum. Each time is more intense than the last, his possession of me more complete. By the time he finally lets me go, I'm deliciously sore, my body humming with satisfaction.

He gets my phone number and makes me promise to see him the next day after work.

I already can't wait.

two

· · ·

Zander

I CAN'T STOP THINKING about her. Chrissy. The memory of her curves, her scent, her soft skin haunts me as I lie in bed, still tasting her on my lips. The way she melted into my arms, surrendering completely. My body aches to possess her again.

I know I came on strong, claiming her as mine. But I don't regret it. She *is* mine now, whether she realizes it yet or not. I've never wanted anyone or anything the way I want her.

My cock throbs insistently as I replay the delicious memories in my mind. The way her cheeks flushed prettily when I whispered filthy promises in her ear. How she trembled and gasped as I slowly peeled her costume off, revealing inch after tantalizing inch of soft, creamy skin. I can still feel the heat of her slick folds enveloping me as I claimed her for the first time, stretching her, marking her as mine. The tender flesh yielding to my hardness. Her tiny whimpers and breathy moans as I moved within her, stoking the flames higher and higher until she shattered apart, sobbing my name.

I grasp my rigid length, stroking firmly from base to tip. I imagine all the wicked, depraved things I want to do to her. Tying her up and teasing her for hours until she's desperate and begging. Bending her over my desk and spanking that delectable ass until it's rosy red. Burying my face between her thighs and feasting on her sweetness until she screams. Making her get on her knees and choking on my cock. The possibilities are endless and I want to do it all, to ruin her for anyone else.

My hand moves faster, urgency building as I picture her pretty lips stretched around me, looking up at me with those innocent doe eyes. Saliva dripping down her chin as she gags and struggles to take it all. I'd fuck her face until tears streamed down her cheeks. Use all her holes ruthlessly for my pleasure.

But I'd take care of her too. Worship every inch of her lush body with my mouth and hands. Bring her to the heights of ecstasy over and over. Cherish her and ensure all her needs and desires are met. Shower her with affection and gifts. Make her feel like the goddess she is.

Pleasure coils tighter and tighter in my core, my shaft pulsing and leaking. I imagine painting her porcelain skin with my seed, marking my territory. My balls draw up tight and with a strangled groan, I erupt. Thick ropes of cum shoot out, splattering my chest and abs. I milk every last drop from my twitching member, shuddering and panting.

As I come down from my high, I know one thing with absolute certainty—I *will* have her again. And again. *Forever*.

Chrissy belongs to *me* now.

My phone buzzes, dragging me from my reverie. Time to face another day as the cutthroat CEO. But first...

I type out a text to Christine:

> Good luck on your first day, beautiful. You'll be amazing.

My driver is already waiting as I hurry out the

door, my thoughts still consumed by her. It's only when I'm settled in the backseat that it hits me—I never asked where she's starting her new job. The realization gnaws at me as we weave through traffic.

The moment I'm in my office, I fire off another text:

> Where are you working now? I want to know everything about you.

I stare at the screen, willing her to respond immediately. My fingers drum impatiently on the desk. I need to know. I crave every detail about her life, her hopes, her fears.

"Mr. Shaw, your 9 AM is here," my assistant's voice crackles through the intercom.

I barely hear her. All I can think about is Chrissy. Her laugh, her smile, the way she fit so perfectly in my arms. I'm utterly obsessed, and I don't care. That sweet, perfect girl is mine, and I'll move heaven and earth to keep her.

Chrissy

I take a deep breath as I step through the gleaming glass doors of Shaw Enterprises. The lobby bustles with activity, a sea of suits and clicking heels against polished marble. My heart races, a mix of excitement and nerves coursing through me.

"Chrissy Harper?" A petite woman with a bright smile approaches. "I'm Melanie from HR. Welcome aboard!"

I shake her hand, grateful for the warm welcome. "Thank you. I'm thrilled to be here."

Melanie leads me through a maze of cubicles and corner offices, introducing me to a blur of new faces. I try to memorize names, but they slip away in my nervous haze.

"And this," Melanie says, gesturing to a sleek desk near a large window, "is your new home away from home."

I run my fingers along the smooth surface, drinking in the view of the city skyline. "It's perfect," I breathe.

As I settle in, arranging my few personal items, my phone buzzes. My stomach flutters when I see Erik's name on the screen. His message makes me smile:

> Where are you working now? I want to know everything about you.

I'm about to type a response when a tall man in an impeccable suit approaches. "Ms. Harper? Mr. Shaw would like to see you in his office immediately."

My fingers freeze over the keyboard. "The CEO wants to see me? Now?"

The man nods, his expression unreadable. "Right this way, please."

I swallow hard, following him towards the imposing double doors at the end of the hall. My phone, with Erik's unanswered text, sits forgotten on my new desk. I knew I would have to meet the CEO of the company sometime, but I'm suddenly a bundle of nerves. I know his HR team hired me, but he certainly has the power to fire me if he doesn't like me.

The suited man deposits me outside a door and nods before walking away.

I take a moment to take a deep breath and collect myself before I step into the office, my heart pounding against my ribs like a caged bird.

The room is bathed in soft light from floor-to-ceiling windows, the city sprawling beneath us. My eyes are drawn to the broad-shouldered silhouette standing with his back to me, gazing out at the skyline.

"Mr. Shaw?" My voice comes out as a whisper, barely audible over the gentle hum of the air conditioning.

He turns, and the world stops spinning.

Those piercing eyes. That chiseled jaw. The same commanding presence that had me spellbound at the Halloween party. It's him. My Phantom. *Erik.*

No. Not Erik. Apparently, he's Zander Shaw. CEO of the company I've just joined.

And my new boss.

"Chrissy," he blinks, obviously just as surprised as I am, but my name still rolls off his tongue like honey.

He seems to collect himself before I do because he smiles a wide, delighted grin. "Welcome to Shaw Industries."

I can't breathe. Can't move. Can't *think.* The room seems to tilt on its axis as I struggle to reconcile the man before me with the enigmatic stranger from the party and the charming texter I've been falling for.

"You..." I manage to choke out. "You're..."

A slow smile spreads across his face. "I had no idea you were my new hire." He's obviously delighted by this turn of events, but I'm not.

I have to work with this man. He's my boss. My boss! This is a disaster.

"I thought your name was Erik," I whisper, my mind reeling. How is this possible? How could I not have known? Why the fuck didn't I look up a picture of my future boss? Surely there are pics of him on the internet. I'm a fucking idiot.

"That's my middle name," he admits sheepishly. "I was caught up in the moment last night." My cheeks burn at his mention of last night. "I was going to tell you my first name today when we talked later after work." His eyes smolder at me. "I had no idea we'd be talking so soon, though."

He takes a step closer, and I catch a whiff of his intoxicating cologne. "I must admit, I'm rather pleased by this turn of events. I'll get to see you all day…"

I want to laugh. I want to cry. I want to run. But I'm rooted to the spot, captivated by his intense gaze.

"Mr. Shaw, I...I don't know what to say."

He reaches out, his fingers brushing my arm, sending electricity coursing through my veins. "Call me Zander."

I swallow.

He takes another step closer to me when I don't speak. "Say my name, Chrissy," his voice is soft and full of that same seduction I couldn't resist last night.

"Zander," I finally say.

He groans, and I can clearly see the prominent outline of his erection in his pants.

Oh lord.

three

. . .

Zander

I WATCH Chrissy saunter into my office, her curves accentuated by that form-fitting pencil skirt. My eyes linger on the sway of her hips, desire coiling in my gut. The scent of her perfume—jasmine and vanilla—fills my senses as she approaches my desk.

"The quarterly reports, Mr. Shaw," she says crisply, placing a stack of folders before me.

Her professional tone only fuels my hunger. I rise slowly, circling my desk until I'm standing mere inches from her. "Thank you, Chrissy," I murmur, my voice low and husky. "But I think we both know that's not why you're really here."

A hint of pink tinges her cheeks, but she holds my gaze. "I'm not sure what you mean."

I lean in closer, drinking in the sight of her parted lips, the rapid rise and fall of her chest. "Don't play coy with me. I see the way you look at me when you think I'm not watching. The spark in your eyes, the hitch in your breath." My fingers graze her arm, feeling her shiver at my touch. "I want you, Chrissy. *Again.*" Fuck, I love the way her cheeks turn pink at the reminder of Halloween night. The night that changed everything for me. "And I know you want me too."

The air between us crackles with electricity. I can almost taste the desire radiating off her in waves. Unable to resist any longer, I pull her into my arms, crushing her soft curves against my chest.

"God, Chrissy," I groan, burying my face in her hair. "I can't stop thinking about you. About that night. The way you felt, the sounds you made." My hands roam her back, memorizing every dip and curve. "Tell me you feel it too. This connection between us."

Her breath comes in short gasps, her fingers clutching at my shirt. I pull back just enough to look into her eyes, seeing my own hunger reflected there. The world narrows to just the two of us, suspended in this moment of unbridled want.

For a moment, Chrissy melts into my embrace, her body molding against mine as if we were made for each other. I can feel her heart racing, matching the frantic beat of my own. But just as I'm about to claim her lips, she stiffens and pulls back, her eyes wide with conflicting emotions.

"Zander, we can't," she whispers, her voice trembling. "This...us...it's not professional." She takes a step back, wrapping her arms around herself as if to ward off the chill of separation. "I've worked so hard to get here, to prove myself. I don't want anyone thinking I got this job by...by sleeping with the boss."

Her words hit me like a bucket of ice water, dousing the fire of my desire. I frown, studying her face. The determination I admire in her is there, but so is a flicker of uncertainty, of longing.

"Chrissy," I say, my voice low and intense. "You're *mine*. I meant what I said before, and I'm not going to let you go." I reach out, cupping her face in my hands. "Your talent, your drive—that's why you're here. Anyone who thinks otherwise is a fool."

She bites her lip, her resolve visibly wavering. "But the rumors, the gossip..."

"Let them talk," I growl, pulling her closer again. "I don't give a damn what anyone else thinks. All I care about is you, *us*." My thumbs caress her cheeks, feeling the warmth of her blush. "I'm not letting go of the best thing that's ever happened to me, professionally or personally."

I can feel her resolve crumbling, her body softening against mine. But then, with a sharp intake of breath, Chrissy takes another step back. The loss of her warmth is immediate, leaving me aching.

"Zander, please," she whispers, her voice a mix of desire and desperation.

I'm not ready to give up. In one fluid motion, I close the distance between us, grasping her hand. The softness of her skin ignites something primal within me. Without breaking eye contact, I guide her palm downward, pressing it firmly against the unmistakable bulge in my trousers.

A small gasp escapes her lips, her eyes widening. I can see the conflict raging within her—the professional mask she wears so diligently threatening to crack under the weight of her desire.

"Feel what you do to me," I murmur, my voice husky with need. "This is real, Chrissy. *We're* real."

Her fingers twitch against me, and I bite back a groan. The air between us is electric, and I *need* her to break. Fuck, I need *her*. For a moment, time stands still, and I dare to hope...

A sharp knock at the door shatters the tension. Chrissy jumps back as if burned, her cheeks flushed crimson. Frustration courses through me, hot and visceral. I turn towards the door, ready to unleash my irritation on whoever dared to interrupt us.

"Mr. Shaw?" a muffled voice calls from the other side.

I glance back at Chrissy, but she's already moving, her professional mask firmly back in place. As the door swings open, she slips past our intruder, disappearing down the hall without a backward glance.

"Get out!" I bark at my innocent employee. His eyes widen. "Later!" I bark.

He obeys without a word, and I should feel bad about how I've just treated one of my best employees, but I don't give a fuck because the unquenched desire coursing through me is visceral.

Left alone, I clench my fists, the ghost of her touch still lingering.

This isn't over, not by a long shot.

four

. . .

Chrissy

MY PHONE BUZZES as I settle onto my couch, exhaling after another grueling day at the office. Zander's name flashes on the screen and my pulse quickens. I slide my finger across to read the message.

> You looked stunning in that dress today. I couldn't take my eyes off you.

Heat rushes to my cheeks. I type back carefully.

> Thank you, but as I mentioned, it's best we keep things professional at work.

The reply is instant.

> Come on Chrissy, we both know there's more between us. Let me take you to dinner, spoil you a little.

I bite my lip, conflicted. His charm is magnetic, but the risks loom large.

> I appreciate the offer, but I must decline. Goodnight, Zander.

I set the phone down with a shaky breath, willing myself not to check for a response. Minutes stretch on agonizingly. At last, I drift into a restless sleep.

A sharp knock startles me awake. Disoriented, I stumble to the door and peer through the peephole. Zander stands outside, devastatingly handsome in a tailored suit. Panic seizes me. How did he find out where I live?

Oh wait. He's my employer. Of course, he knows where I live.

Bracing myself, I crack open the door. "Zander, what are you doing here? It's late."

His eyes smolder at me as he leans against the doorframe. "I wanted to see you. May I come in?"

"I don't think that's a good idea." My words sound feeble even to my own ears.

Zander's steps closer, his expensive cologne enveloping me. "Chrissy, I know everything about you. What you like, what you want." His voice drops to a sensual murmur. "The way you melt under my gaze in the office when you think no one's watching."

I swallow hard, heart pounding in my ears. The temptation to surrender is overwhelming. But the fear of jeopardizing everything I've worked for wars within me.

His fingertips graze my cheek, igniting sparks under my skin...

In a daze, I step aside, allowing him entrance. The door closes with a resounding click.

Zander immediately backs me against the wall, his body pinning mine. His lips descend on mine, hungry and demanding. I melt into the kiss, trying in vain to keep my wits about me.

He pulls away, trailing kisses along my jawline. "You belong to me, Chrissy. You know it. I know it."

I try to protest, but my words are lost in a moan as his hands find their way under my negligee. He knowingly caresses my swollen folds, eliciting a shudder.

"Zander, we can't...we're...boss...employee..." My voice trails off as his skilled fingers tease me closer to the edge.

"Shh...I've got you," he soothes, his voice gravelly with arousal.

I arch my back, lost in the sensations coursing through me. He captures my moans with his mouth, expertly prolonging my pleasure.

"Chrissy," he growls, pulling away. "I've wanted this all fucking day."

Before I can react, he's unzipped his pants, his thick cock pulsing in front of me. I gasp, his size and power causing a delicious shiver down my spine.

"No, Zander...we should...we can't..."

He silences me with a finger to my lips. "You've been driving me crazy since the day I laid eyes on you. Tonight, you're mine. All mine."

His words send a thrill through me, despite my better judgment. Taking my hand, he guides it to his erection, his heat searing my skin.

"Touch yourself, Chrissy. Show me how much you want this."

My cheeks burn, but I obey, unable to deny the

hunger in his eyes. I slide my fingers over my wet folds, coating them in my juices.

"That's my girl," he growls, his need palpable.

Without warning, he positions himself between my legs, guiding his cock to my entrance. My protests die on my lips as he slides inch by aching inch inside me. Heat pools deep within me, melting my resistance.

"Feel that, Chrissy? That's how perfect we are together."

He's right...God, I hate that he's right.

As he moves inside me, slowly at first, then faster and harder, I can't deny the passion that rages between us. In Zander's arms, I've never felt more alive.

He angles his hips, hitting that spot deep within me, and I cry out. I'm so close, so...

"Come for me, Chrissy. Come on my cock," he growls in my ear, his voice dark and commanding.

That's all I need.

My orgasm washes over me like a tidal wave, crashing against the shore of my senses. My body arches, my moans echoing in the dimly lit office. I grip onto his broad shoulders, my nails digging into his skin as ecstasy melts my bones. Zander grunts, and I feel his hot release inside me, sealing our union.

As our breathing eases, we stay entwined, our hearts racing in tandem. In the aftermath, the weight of our actions settles upon me like a heavy blanket. "You need to go," I whisper as I step back from him.

"Chrissy," he growls in protest.

"We have work in the morning," I remind him. "And it's late."

He clenches his jaw shut tight before he tucks himself back into his pants and turns to leave. But then he turns back and kisses me soundly before whispering "You're mine, you beautiful girl," against my lips.

When I close the door behind him, I slump back against, my knees no longer to hold me up in the wake of the storm that is Zander.

five

. . .

Chrissy

I STARE INTENTLY at my computer screen, trying to lose myself in the intricate details of Zander's schedule for the upcoming week. The cursor blinks, taunting me with each passing second. His presence lingers at the edges of my consciousness, a constant distraction despite my best efforts to avoid him.

The door to my office swings open and Zander strides in, his tailored suit hugging his lean frame in all the right places. My breath catches in my throat as our eyes meet, a startling jolt of electricity passing between us.

"Chrissy, I need the quarterly reports on my desk by noon," he says, his deep voice sending shivers down my spine.

I nod, not trusting myself to speak. His gaze lingers a moment too long before he turns and leaves, the air still crackling with tension in his wake.

With shaking hands, I return to my work, determined to push thoughts of Zander from my mind. But it's a futile effort. He's everywhere—in the spicy scent of his cologne that clings to the air, in the ghost of his touch on my skin from accidental brushes in the hallway.

A soft knock at the door jolts me from my reverie. I glance up to see Zander's assistant, a knowing smile playing at the corners of her lips as she hands me a small, elegantly wrapped box.

"From Zander," she says simply before disappearing.

With trembling fingers, I open the gift to reveal a stunning silver bracelet, the delicate links glinting in the fluorescent light of my office. A note flutters out, Zander's bold script searing into my mind.

"A token of my appreciation for all your hard work. Wear it and think of me. - Z"

My heart races as I clasp the bracelet around my wrist, the cool metal a constant reminder of his presence. I shouldn't accept it, shouldn't encourage whatever this is between us. But I can't bring myself to take it off.

As I lose myself once more in the monotony of spreadsheets and emails, Zander's face swims before my eyes, his heated gaze promising things I dare not even imagine. Each keystroke becomes a battle, a desperate attempt to maintain the professional distance I know we need.

But with every passing day, every stolen glance and secret gift, I feel my resolve crumbling. Zander Shaw is a force to be reckoned with, and I fear I may be powerless to resist his charms much longer.

***

The glittering lights of the ballroom dance across my skin as I weave through the crowd, my heart beating in time with the soft jazz that fills the air. This is a company affair, a charity gala, that Zander demanded we all attend.

I'm no idiot. I know why. He wasn't going to give me a chance to get away from him.

I can feel Zander's presence like a physical touch, his eyes tracking my every move from across the room.

I take a steadying breath, smoothing my hands over the rich fabric of my gown. It clings to my curves like a second skin, the deep crimson hue a stark contrast to my usual conservative attire. A daring choice, but one that makes me feel powerful, desirable.

As if drawn by an invisible force, Zander materializes at my side, his hand grazing the small of my back. Electricity crackles between us, the heat of his touch searing through the thin silk.

"You look stunning," he murmurs, his breath hot against my ear. "I can't take my eyes off you."

I flush, my skin tingling with awareness. "Zander, we can't..."

But he's already leading me onto the dance floor, his arm sliding around my waist as he pulls me close. The scent of his cologne envelops me, rich and intoxicating, as we begin to move in perfect sync.

"Just one dance," he whispers, his lips brushing the shell of my ear. "Let me have this moment with you."

I close my eyes, letting the music wash over me as Zander guides me across the floor. His touch is electric, his body molding to mine as if we were made for each other. The world falls away until there's nothing but the two of us, lost in the rhythm of our own private melody.

As the song draws to a close, Zander's hand lingers on my hip, his thumb tracing slow circles that send shivers down my spine. I know I should pull away, put some distance between us before someone notices. But I can't seem to make myself move, caught in the web of his intense gaze.

"Meet me on the balcony in five minutes," he breathes, his voice low and urgent. "I need to talk to you alone."

Then he's gone, melting into the crowd like a phantom. I stand frozen, my heart racing as I try to gather my scattered thoughts. The rational part of me knows I should ignore his request, maintain the professional boundaries I've fought so hard to establish.

But the ache in my chest, the yearning that's been building with every stolen moment and secret touch, propels me forward. Before I can second-guess myself, I'm slipping through the French doors, the cool night air a balm against my flushed skin.

Zander's already waiting, his silhouette outlined against the twinkling city lights. He turns as I approach, his eyes darkening with an emotion I can't quite name.

"Chrissy," he says softly, reaching out to tuck a stray curl behind my ear. His fingers linger, tracing the delicate line of my jaw. "I can't keep pretending that I don't feel this...this connection between us."

I swallow hard, my pulse thundering in my ears. "Zander, we can't do this. You're my boss, and I've worked too hard to jeopardize my career."

"I know," he sighs, his forehead resting against mine. "But I can't ignore what's happening here. Can you honestly tell me you don't feel it too?"

His words hang in the air between us, heavy with unspoken desire. I know I should deny it, push him away and retreat to the safety of my carefully constructed walls.

But as Zander's lips hover a mere breath from mine, his hand curving possessively around my hip, I realize I'm tired of fighting this irresistible pull. Consequences be damned, I want to surrender to the fire that's been smoldering between us for far too long.

My eyes flutter closed, my body swaying instinctively toward his. "Zander," I whisper, my voice barely audible over the pounding of my heart. "Please..."

With that single word, all pretense of restraint shatters. Zander's mouth crushes against mine, his kiss hungry, consuming, as if he has been waiting for this moment as long as I have. His tongue traces my lower lip, seeking entry, and I can't help but part my lips for him.

The taste of him is intoxicating, his touch

igniting a fire that burns hotter than any November flame. I'm lost in the storm of sensations as he deepens the kiss, his hands roaming my curves with a possessiveness that should terrify me.

But instead, I'm consumed by a need I've never before experienced, my body melting into his as if we were always meant to be together. The tension that has been simmering between us for days finally boils over, and I find myself clinging to him, desperate for more.

Our hands are everywhere, exploring, cataloging, our clothes seeming to melt away as we yield to the heat between us. It's only when our hands brush against the cold concrete wall that we both freeze, reality crashing down around us like unrelenting rain.

I pull away, gasping for air, my heart pounding in my ears. "Zander, we...we shouldn't have done that." I can't meet his eyes, and I know my cheeks are aflame.

"Why not?" he growls, his voice a low rumble in his chest. "You felt as good in my arms as I did having you in them."

"Because...because we work together, and...and it's inappropriate." I can hear the desperation in my voice, but I can't seem to stop myself from making excuses.

Zander's laugh is harsh, bouncing off the walls of our dark sanctuary. "Inappropriate? Chrissy, I'm the damn boss, and I don't give a fuck. It's not like you're going to get fired. I won't allow it."

He's right, of course. But I can't admit that out loud, not to him, not when everything is so raw and vulnerable between us.

"But that's just it, Zander! People find out about us, and all my hard work is undermined. I'll become the girl who slept her way to the top. Please, we have to forget about all this." I gather my composure, straightening my clothes and wiping the remnants of our passion from my lips, though my voice sounds unconvincing even to my own ears.

"Can we?" His voice is dangerously soft, sending shivers down my spine. "I don't think I can forget the way you felt in my arms, the way you taste...I've waited too long for this, Chrissy. I'm not giving you up now."

The intensity in his eyes sends a shiver down my spine, and I can feel myself wavering. "Zander, we can't...it's...it's just...so..."

"Wrong?" his voice is an angry growl in my ear as he steps closer, his warmth enveloping me once again. "I don't know about you, but that felt pretty damn right to me." His fingers brush against my cheek, sending electricity through my veins. "Don't you ever say that we're wrong, Chrissy. Nothing is this fucking world is more right."

I step back abruptly, my chest heaving with the effort to regain control. "No, Zander. We can't do this. Not here, not now."

Zander's eyes flash with frustration, his jaw clenching as he runs a hand through his tousled hair. "Why not, Chrissy? Why can't we just give in to what we both want?"

"Because it's not that simple!" I snap, my voice trembling with barely suppressed emotion. "I have worked too hard to get where I am, and I won't risk it all for a fleeting moment of passion."

He steps closer, his presence overwhelming in the intimate space. "Who says it has to be fleeting? Chrissy, I want more than just a moment with you."

I close my eyes, fighting the temptation to melt into his arms and forget the world outside. But the nagging voice of reason persists, reminding me of the potential consequences.

"I can't, Zander. Please, don't make this harder than it already is." My words are a whispered plea, a desperate attempt to hold onto the last shreds of my resolve.

Zander's chest heaves up and down, and he

looks like an overheated bull that's about to gore someone.

He finally steps back, the cool night air rushing between us like a physical barrier. I wrap my arms around myself, suddenly feeling chilled to the bone.

"I should go," I murmur, turning to leave before I can change my mind.

As I walk away, I feel Zander's gaze burning into my back, the unspoken words hanging heavy in the air. My heart aches with each step, torn between the desire to turn back and the knowledge that I must keep moving forward.

The journey home passes in a blur, my mind replaying the events of the evening in an endless loop. By the time I reach my apartment, I'm exhausted, emotionally drained, and more confused than ever.

I sink onto my couch, burying my face in my hands as the tears finally come. I'm angry at myself for letting things go this far, angry at Zander for making me feel things I've tried so hard to suppress.

But beneath the anger is a yearning so deep it takes my breath away. I want Zander with every fiber of my being, even as I know that pursuing this relationship could be my undoing.

As I sit in the darkness, the weight of my decision pressing down on me, I realize that I can't keep running from my feelings. I need to set clear boundaries, to make Zander understand that our professional lives must remain separate from any personal connection we may share.

But even as I make this resolution, I know that my heart isn't fully on board. Because no matter how hard I try to fight it, Zander has already claimed a piece of my soul that I fear I may never get back.

six

. . .

Zander

I KNOCK FIRMLY on Chrissy's apartment door, my heart pounding in rhythm with my fist. The cool night air does little to calm the heat simmering beneath my skin. I need to see her. *Now*.

The door swings open and there she stands, her hazel eyes wide with surprise. "Zander? What are you doing here?"

My gaze rakes over her, drinking in the sight I've been craving for weeks. The soft curves of her body are draped in a silky robe that clings in all the right places. Desire coils tight in my gut.

"I had to see you," I say, my voice low and

rough with need. "I can't stand this distance between us anymore."

Chrissy bites her plump lower lip, uncertainty warring with longing in her eyes. After a charged moment, she steps back and gestures for me to come inside. The apartment is dimly lit, shadows dancing on the walls. The air feels heavy, weighted with unspoken desires.

I follow her into the living room, my body gravitating towards hers like a magnet. She turns to face me and I can't tear my gaze away from her. The way the robe frames her figure is mesmerizing. I ache to run my hands over her soft skin, to claim her mouth with my own.

"Zander, we can't keep doing this," Chrissy whispers, but there's no conviction in her voice.

I step closer, until mere inches separate us. Her intoxicating scent wraps around me, fueling my need. "I don't care about anything else. I only care about you."

My fingertips graze her cheek, trailing down the elegant column of her neck. Her pulse jumps beneath my touch and a shaky breath escapes her parted lips. The sexual tension crackling between us is a living thing, threatening to consume us both.

"Tell me you don't feel this too," I murmur, my

thumb brushing over her full lower lip. "Tell me you don't want me as badly as I want you."

Chrissy's eyes flutter closed for a brief moment before locking with mine again, dark with desire. "I do, Zander. But..."

I silence her protests with a searing kiss, pouring every ounce of pent-up passion into the press of my lips against hers. She melts into me, her hands fisting in my shirt as a needy moan rises in her throat. I deepen the kiss, my tongue tangling with hers in a sensual dance. My hands map the curves of her body, desperate to touch and explore.

We stumble backwards until Chrissy's back hits the wall. I cage her in with my arms, my body fitting perfectly against her soft curves. Her robe has slipped off one shoulder, revealing creamy skin that begs to be tasted. I trail open-mouthed kisses down her neck, reveling in the little gasps of pleasure that escape her.

"Zander, please..." Chrissy breathes, her nails digging into my shoulders. "We shouldn't..."

But her body arches into mine, betraying her true desires. I capture her mouth again, silencing any further protests. In this moment, nothing exists except the scorching heat between us, the overwhelming need to make her mine. Consequences be damned. All that matters is the feeling of her skin against mine, the way she trembles under my touch.

I'm lost in her, drowning in the depths of my desire for this incredible woman. And I never want to come up for air.

My hands find the tie of Chrissy's robe, tugging it loose. The silky fabric parts like water, revealing her lush curves clad only in a thin nightgown. My breath catches at the sight—she is a vision of sensual beauty in the dim light. I want to worship every inch of her body.

"I'm going to take care of every beautiful inch of you, baby," I tell her, my voice rough with awe. "Give that pussy everything it needs.

Chrissy's eyes are dark with desire as she gazes up at me. Her hands work at the buttons of my shirt with desperate urgency. "I need you, Zander. I can't fight this anymore..."

"Then don't," I growl, shrugging out of my shirt and pulling her flush against my bare chest. "Let me love you, Chrissy. Let me show you how good we can be together."

I capture her mouth in a searing kiss, pouring all my longing and frustration into the slant of our lips. Chrissy matches my passion, her tongue dancing with mine as her hands map my shoulders, my back. I groan into her mouth when her nails rake lightly over my skin.

Driven by a primal urge to claim her, I hoist Chrissy up, encouraging her legs to wrap around my waist. She gasps at the bold move, fingers clutching at my shoulders for balance. I can feel the heat of her core through the thin barrier of her panties, stoking my arousal to a fever pitch.

Chrissy breaks the kiss with a moan as I grind against her. "Bedroom," she pants, eyes glazed with need.

I carry her down the hall, our mouths fused in deep, drugging kisses. The rest of our clothing is dispatched in a flurry of grasping hands and whispered pleas. By the time we tumble onto the bed, we are skin to skin, nothing left between us.

I take a moment to drink in the sight of Chrissy laid out before me, all creamy curves and soft skin. My hands skim reverently over her body, committing every dip and swell to memory.

Chrissy arches into my touch, a breathy moan escaping her kiss-swollen lips. "Please, Zander," she whimpers, desperation coloring her tone. "I need you inside me."

"Fuck yes, that's what I'm talking about." Seeing her wanting me like this has me going insane. I kiss her as I settle between her parted thighs, the heat of her core scorching against my aching flesh. With agonizing slowness, I ease into her slick depths, groaning at the exquisite feeling of her body welcoming me home.

Chrissy cries out, nails digging into my shoulders as I fill her completely.

"God, you feel incredible," I rasp against the shell of her ear, punctuating my words with a deep, languid thrust. "So tight. So perfect."

Chrissy rolls her hips to meet mine, urging me deeper. Our bodies find a primal rhythm, rocking together in a sensual give and take. Soft sighs and reverent touches mingle with breathless pleas and grasping hands. We lose ourselves in the push and pull of our joining, climbing higher with each fevered slide of skin against skin.

I place my hands on either side of her face and force her to look into my eyes. "I'm not just fucking you, baby. You understand that? I'm making love to you. You stop fighting us. You understand me? I'm going to take care of everything."

Chrissy whimpers, her inner muscles fluttering around my surging length. "Don't stop, please don't stop..."

I capture her mouth in a searing kiss once more, swallowing her cries of ecstasy as I drive into her with abandon. My own release coils tight at the base of my spine, white-hot tendrils of pleasure spiraling through my veins. With a hoarse shout, I empty myself deep inside her welcoming heat, her name a reverent chant on my lips.

We cling to each other as the aftershocks slowly fade, hearts pounding in sync. I trail tender kisses over Chrissy's face, brushing damp strands of hair from her flushed cheeks. In this perfect moment, everything else fades away. All that remains is the undeniable rightness of her body entwined with mine.

"Stay with me tonight," Chrissy murmurs, her eyes soft and vulnerable in the muted light. "I don't want to let you go just yet."

I gather her close, savoring the feel of her curves molding to my harder planes. "Wild horses couldn't drag me away," I promise, sealing my vow with a slow, deep kiss.

———

The gray light of dawn filters through the curtains as I slowly blink awake, momentarily disoriented. The events of last night come rushing back—Zander's unexpected arrival, our explosive argument that morphed into something else entirely. The ache between my thighs and the warm, solid presence at my back serve as undeniable proof that it wasn't just a vivid dream.

Panic claws at my throat as the reality of the situation sinks in. I slept with Zander. Again.

My career, my reputation...everything I've worked so hard for could be ruined if this gets out. The thoughts sour the blissful afterglow.

I try to slip out of bed without waking Zander, desperate for some space to clear my head and figure out how to handle this mess. But the moment I sit up, his arm snakes around my waist, tugging me back against his chest.

"Where do you think you're going?" he murmurs, nuzzling into the crook of my neck. His voice is still rough from sleep, sending shivers down my spine.

"I...we...," I stammer, trying to ignore the way my body instinctively melts into his. "If anyone at work finds out-"

"Stop." Zander's fingers press gently against my lips, halting my anxious spiral. He shifts so he can look me in the eye, his gaze intense but tender. "I know you care about proving your worth at work, and your work ethic is one of the many things I admire about you, but stop worrying, beautiful. I don't care what anyone thinks, Chrissy. I want this. I want you."

My heart stutters in my chest at his words, equal parts thrilled and terrified. "But our careers," I whisper. "The gossip, the accusations of favoritism..."

"We'll handle it," he says firmly. "Together. I'm not going to let narrow-minded busybodies stand in the way of something this real." His thumb strokes along my cheekbone, his touch grounding me. "I'm all in, Chrissy. Professionally, personally...in every way. If you'll have me."

Tears prick at the backs of my eyes as a tentative hope unfurls in my chest. Could we really make this work? The logical part of my brain throws up a dozen red flags, but my heart is already leaping ahead, daring to imagine a future where I don't have to choose between love and ambition.

I hesitate, my heart torn between the undeniable pull toward Zander and the fear of jeopardizing everything I've worked so hard for. The morning light filtering through the curtains casts a soft glow on his chiseled features, making him look almost ethereal. I take a deep breath, steeling myself for the words I know I have to say.

"Zander, I..." My voice catches, and I clear my throat. "I think we need to keep things strictly professional at work. At least for now."

His brow furrows, a flicker of hurt crossing his

face before he smooths it away. "I understand your concerns, Chrissy. But I don't want to hide this—hide us."

I reach out, taking his hand in mine, marveling at how perfectly they fit together even though his is so much bigger than mine. "I don't want to hide either. But the thought of people gossiping, the backlash it could cause... I've worked too hard to let anything tarnish my reputation."

Zander searches my eyes. "Why are you so worried about this?"

I try to look away, but Zander won't allow it. He grabs my chin and forces me to meet his gaze. He knows there's more to it than I've been letting on.

I exhale and finally confess, "My mom slept with her boss, and people always gave her shit about it. Hell, they gave me shit about it too. I don't want to be like that."

Zander's thumb traces soothing circles on the back of my hand, his touch both comforting and electrifying as his eyes soften with understanding. "Why didn't you just tell me that from the start?"

I shrug. "It's not exactly the sort of thing I'm proud of." Zander is silent for a long moment before he concedes, "We'll be discreet. Keep our personal life separate from work. But I don't want to pretend that this never happened, that it doesn't mean anything."

I bite my lip, torn between the desire to throw caution to the wind and the deeply ingrained need to protect myself. "It means everything to me, Zander. You mean everything to me."

He pulls me into his arms, my head fitting perfectly into the crook of his neck. I breathe in his scent, a heady mix of sandalwood and something uniquely him. "We'll take it slow. Figure it out together. But I'm not going anywhere, Chrissy. I'm in this for the long haul. You're mine, baby."

Tears prick at the corners of my eyes, and I blink them back, overwhelmed by the depth of emotion in his words. "Okay," I whisper, my decision made. "We'll keep it professional at work. But when we're alone..."

Zander's lips curve into a wicked grin, his eyes darkening with promise. "When we're alone, all bets are off."

He captures my mouth in a searing kiss, and I melt into him, my doubts and fears dissolving as he shows me once again just what we're going to do every time we're alone.

seven

. . .

Chrissy

I CATCH a glimpse of Zander through the glass walls of the conference room, his charismatic presence commanding the attention of everyone at the table. My heart skips a beat, memories of our passionate encounters flooding my mind. Shaking my head, I try to refocus on the report in front of me, but the words blur together.

"Chrissy, I need those projections by noon," Zander's voice cuts through my thoughts as he strides past my desk, the scent of his cologne lingering in the air.

"Of course, Mr. Shaw," I reply, my tone professional despite the flush creeping up my neck. "I'll have them ready."

His gaze lingers on me for a moment too long, a hint of a smile playing at the corners of his lips. "Excellent. And Chrissy..."

He leans in closer, his breath hot against my ear. "I can't stop thinking about last night."

I swallow hard, trying to ignore the heat pooling in my belly. "Zander, we can't... not here."

"Meet me in my office at lunch. We need to talk." His tone leaves no room for argument.

As he walks away, I feel the weight of curious eyes on me. Whispers follow in his wake, speculations about the nature of our relationship. I bury myself in work, desperate to quell the rumors before they spiral out of control.

But every time Zander passes by, every stolen glance and brush of his hand against mine, I'm drawn back into the intoxicating web of our forbidden desire. The walls of my carefully constructed professionalism crumble under the force of his ardor.

Lunchtime arrives, and I find myself standing outside Zander's office, heart pounding in my chest. I knock softly, half-hoping he won't answer.

"Come in." His deep voice sends shivers down my spine.

I step inside, closing the door behind me. Zander leans against his desk, arms crossed over his broad chest. "Chrissy, I've been dying to get my hands on these curves all day."

"I thought we agreed…" I whisper, avoiding his intense gaze.

"I understand your worries, honey, but I got you," He closes the distance between us, tilting my chin up to meet his eyes. "I want to be with you, Chrissy. No more secrets, no more hiding."

"Zander…" Tears prick at the corners of my eyes.

He sighs, frustration etched into the lines of his handsome face.

He grabs my hand and places it on his crotch. "I am constantly hard for you, baby."

Heat flares between my thighs and I bite my lip.

He groans and pulls his cock out.

"Zander," I hiss. "We can't. Not here."

But he isn't listening to me. He hoists me up on his desk, pushes my skirt up and spreads my legs. Then, oh god, he roughly pushes my panties to the side and starts to lick me.

And oh. My. *God.*

I grip the desk, my head rolling back as he eats me out, jacking his cock off the entire time.

His tongue swirls around my clit, flicking and teasing, sending electric shockwaves of pleasure radiating through my body. I moan softly, trying to stifle the sounds of my ecstasy, all too aware of the thin walls and bustling office just outside the door.

Zander's fingers dig into my thighs as he devours me, his stubble grazing deliciously against my sensitive skin. The obscene wet noises of his tongue lapping at my slick folds fill the room, mingling with his deep groans of satisfaction.

"Fuck, you taste incredible. Like ripe peaches," he growls against my pussy, the vibrations of his voice making me shudder. His hand pumps faster on his thick shaft, pre-cum glistening at the tip.

I thread my fingers through his dark hair, holding him closer, silently begging for more. He obliges, thrusting his tongue inside me, fucking me with it as his thumb finds my clit. He rubs tight circles, building the pressure higher and higher until I'm writhing beneath his touch.

"That's it, baby. Come on my face. I want to feel you let go," Zander commands, his tone rough with lust.

My thighs start to quake and quiver, my walls clenching around his tongue as the wave of my release crashes over me. I throw my head back, biting my lip hard to contain my cries of pleasure as I come undone, my essence coating his face.

Zander laps up every drop, prolonging my

orgasm until I'm a boneless, trembling mess. With a final kiss to my sensitive clit, he rises to his feet, still stroking his impressive length.

He positions himself between my legs, the head of his cock nudging against my soaked entrance. For a moment, I think he's going to take me right here on his desk, but instead, he begins to paint my pussy with his seed, marking me as his.

I watch in awe as thick ropes of his cum land on my tender flesh, dripping down to soak my panties. Zander milks every last drop from his cock, a wicked gleam in his eye.

"I love knowing my cum will be on you all day, a constant reminder of who you belong to," he smirks, carefully adjusting my panties back into place. The feeling of the damp fabric against my skin is a delicious secret I'll carry with me.

He helps me off the desk, stealing a deep, possessive kiss. I can taste myself on his tongue, a heady reminder of our illicit tryst.

"Back to work, Ms. Harper," Zander winks, giving my ass a playful swat.

I straighten my skirt and smooth my hair, trying to regain some semblance of composure. My legs still feel weak as I make my way to the door, my heart racing with the thrill of what we just did.

I exit Zander's office on shaky legs, my mind

reeling from our heated encounter. The lingering sensation of his mouth on me, his cum marking my most intimate parts, sends a shiver down my spine. I can't help but clench my thighs together, savoring the damp reminder pressed against my skin.

Maybe Zander is right. Maybe I need to stop worrying so much.

eight

· · ·

Chrissy

THE COPY ROOM feels stifling as I fold and collate the endless stacks of reports. The rhythmic hum of the machines fades into the background as my mind wanders to him. *Zander*.

No matter how much I try to focus on work, my traitorous thoughts keep straying to stolen glances across the conference table, the electric tingle when our hands accidentally brush reaching for the same file.

I startle at the sound of a throat clearing behind me. It's not him. Of course not. Turning, I paste on a polite smile for Mark, one of the junior accountants.

"Chrissy, I was wondering..." He shifts his weight nervously. "Would you maybe want to grab dinner sometime? With me?"

My stomach drops. Before I can even begin to formulate a response, a deep, commanding voice cuts through the room.

"That won't be happening." Zander's broad frame fills the doorway, his piercing gaze fixed on Mark. "In fact, you're fired. Clear out your desk immediately."

Mark's face drains of color. He stammers incoherently before scurrying out of the room. I whirl to face Zander, indignation rising.

"What the hell was that? You can't just fire someone for asking me out!"

In two long strides, he's in front of me, his presence overwhelming. "I can and I did. I'm done pretending, Chrissy. You're mine."

His words send a forbidden thrill through me even as I bristle. "You had no right—"

"I had every fucking right!" The rest of my tirade is swallowed by his lips claiming mine in a searing kiss. I should push him away, but instead I melt into him, my hands fisting in his crisp shirt.

He backs me against the copier, his strong thigh pressing between my legs. "I have every right," he growls against my neck. "And I'm going to show you and everyone else that you're mine. No more games."

Buttons fly as he rips open my blouse. I gasp as his scorching mouth blazes a trail down my throat to my heaving breasts. Rational thought scatters. All that exists is his touch igniting my skin.

He hikes up my skirt, shoving my panties aside. I'm already slick and aching. The first thrust of his fingers into my heat has me seeing stars. "This perfect pussy belongs to me. Say it."

"Yes," I whimper, lost to sensation. "I'm yours."

He rewards me by curling his fingers, stoking the fire building low in my belly. I rock against his hand, chasing the shimmering edge of release.

His voice is a dark rumble in my ear. "That's my good girl. I'm going to fuck you now. Right here where anyone could walk in and see who you belong to."

I should be scandalized, but the thought only makes me wetter. I'm panting and needy, dignity discarded, as he frees himself from his slacks and notches his thick length at my entrance.

With one brutal snap of his hips, he's inside me, stretching and filling me so perfectly. I cry out, my nails digging into his shoulders. He sets a punishing pace, his pelvis grinding against my aching clit with each deep stroke.

The copier rattles beneath me as he pounds into my willing body. My head falls back, thighs trembling around his waist. I'm so close, teetering on the knife's edge of agonizing bliss.

"Scream my name when you come," he demands. "Now."

His command sends me hurtling over, my climax crashing through me in dizzying waves of pleasure as I obey him, whining out his name as my pussy convulses around him.

He follows me over the edge, pouring himself into me with a guttural groan of my name.

We stare at one another as we catch our breath before Zander growls, "Now let's make sure everyone knows who you belong to."

He tucks me back into my clothes, doing up the buttons of my blouse with surprising tenderness. But there's no mistaking the possessive grip of his hand at the small of my back as he leads me out to the main office...

Zander's words echo in my mind as we step out of his office, my legs still unsteady. The normally bustling workspace seems to freeze, all eyes drawn to us—to *me*—as if they can see the evidence of our tryst written across my flushed face.

Of course, they probably fucking heard it, thanks to Zander and his commands.

He leans in close, his breath hot against my ear. "If being with you means losing you as my assistant, then so be it. I'll fire you if I have to, Chrissy. I won't let anything stand in the way of us being together."

My heart stutters, a dizzying mix of elation and trepidation swirling through me. This job, this career, has been my driving force for so long. Can I really just let it go? Let him dismiss me so cavalierly?

But as I meet his heated gaze, I realize it's not cavalier at all. There's a fierce sincerity burning in those pewter depths, a promise that he'll burn the world down to keep me by his side. And God help me, I want that. I suddenly realize that I want him more than I want a job or a reputation.

Steeling my resolve, I turn to face him fully, my voice low but steady. "You're right, Zander, and I'm sorry. I'm done running. Done pretending that my heart doesn't race every time you look at me."

His eyes flare with triumph and naked hunger. His hand slides possessively over my hip, staking his claim. "Then we're in agreement. You're mine, Chrissy. The rest is just details."

And as he captures my mouth in a searing kiss, right there in front of everyone, I know he's right. The job, the office politics, the whispers that are sure to follow—none of it matters. Not when I'm in his arms.

I've spent so long chasing the perfect career, the perfect image. But maybe happiness doesn't lie in perfection. Maybe it lies in surrender. In taking a leap and trusting that this complicated, messy, wonderful man will catch me.

His kiss is a vow, a brand. And I wear it proudly.

Zander, ever the confident leader, strides into the main office area with me by his side. His presence commands attention, and all eyes turn to us. I catch sight of the man who had asked me out earlier, his expression a mix of confusion and apprehension.

"Everyone, I have an announcement," Zander's voice rings out, clear and authoritative. "First, I want to apologize to James for my earlier outburst. Your job is secure, and I appreciate your contributions to the team."

James nods, relief evident on his face. But the tension in the room remains palpable, everyone waiting for the other shoe to drop.

Zander's hand tightens around mine, a silent reassurance. "Secondly, I want to make it clear that Chrissy and I are together. She's not just my executive assistant. She's my partner in every sense of the word."

Murmurs ripple through the office, a mix of surprise and speculation. I feel the weight of their stares, the unspoken questions hanging in the air. But with Zander's solid presence beside me, I find the strength to meet their gazes head-on.

Zander expression softens as he looks at me. "Chrissy is an invaluable member of this team, and I'm lucky to have her by my side, both personally and professionally. I hope you'll all support us as we navigate this new chapter."

The room is silent for a heartbeat, then slowly, smiles begin to appear on faces. Some are genuine, others more tentative, but the overall atmosphere feels lighter, more accepting.

As we make our way back to Zander's office, I lean into him, drawing strength from his presence. "That went better than I expected," I murmur.

He chuckles, pressing a kiss to my temple. "They'd be fools to challenge me—especially where you're concerned."

I smile, my heart full to bursting.

"And now, I'm about to give you a raise," he says as he raises an eyebrow at me and pats his lap.

I flush and move to straddle him.

My boss. My lover.

Zander.

epilogue

. . .

Three years later

Zander

I CLOSE the door to my office, locking it behind me with a satisfying click. Chrissy stands before me, her curves hugged by that sinful black dress I love so much. Even after three years of marriage, the hunger for her only grows stronger each day.

"Mr. Shaw," she purrs, running a manicured finger down my chest. "You wanted to see me?"

I grab her wrist, pulling her flush against me. "Always, Mrs. Shaw. I'll never get enough of you."

My hands roam her body possessively as I claim

her mouth in a searing kiss. She melts into me, soft and pliant, her desire matching my own. I lift her onto my desk, shoving aside papers and pens. Nothing else matters when I have my wife in my arms.

I hike up her dress, revealing silky thighs and lacy panties. "You're so sexy, baby. I want to fill this sweet pussy with my cum. Put my baby in your belly."

She moans as I rub her through the damp fabric. "Yes, Zander. I want that too. Want to carry your child."

I nearly rip her panties in my haste to remove them. She helps me unbuckle my belt and release my aching cock. I position myself at her entrance, teasing her slick folds. "Tell me you're mine, Chrissy. Forever."

"I'm yours," she breathes. "Only yours. Always."

With a powerful thrust, I bury myself deep inside her welcoming heat. She cries out in plea- sure, nails digging into my shoulders. I set a relent- less pace, driven by an all-consuming need to claim my wife.

Chrissy's face is flushed, eyes glazed with passion as I take her on my desk. Her hands clutch at me desperately, urging me deeper. I can never resist her, this gorgeous woman who owns my heart so completely.

"That's it, baby," I grunt, pounding into her willing body. "Take my cock. Gonna fill this pussy so full."

She whimpers and writhes beneath me, lost to the pleasure. I feel her walls start to flutter around my shaft and I know she's close. I reach between us, finding her swollen clit. I rub firm circles and she shatters with a keening cry.

"Zander! Oh god, yes!"

Her pussy clenches me like a vice as she comes undone. It's too much, the erotic sight and sensation sending me over the edge. I bury myself to the hilt and explode inside her, marking her womb with my seed.

"Fuck, Chrissy! Take it, baby. All for you," I groan, emptying every last drop.

We stay joined as the aftershocks ripple through us, foreheads pressed together. I pepper her face with soft kisses, savoring the intimacy. She sighs contentedly, snuggling into my embrace.

"I love you, Mr. Shaw," she murmurs against my lips. "More than anything."

"I love you too, Mrs. Shaw. You're my world."

We reluctantly separate and right our clothes. She's always beautiful, but when she's all disheveled from recently being fucked, she takes my breath away. I cup her face tenderly, still in awe that this incredible woman chose me. Chose *us*.

Chrissy bites her lip, eyes sparkling with a secret. She takes my hand and places it low on her stomach.

"Zander...I have something to tell you." She smiles radiantly. "I'm pregnant."

My heart stops, then kicks into overdrive as her words sink in. Pregnant. My wife is pregnant with our child. Joy surges through me, so intense it steals my breath.

"Really? You're sure?" I manage to ask, voice rough with emotion.

She nods, happy tears shimmering in her eyes. "I took a test this morning. We're going to be parents, Zander."

I crush her to me, burying my face in her fragrant hair. "Oh Chrissy. You've made me the happiest man alive. I can't wait to start our family together."

I drop to my knees and press reverent kisses to her still-flat tummy. She threads her fingers through my hair, cradling me close. In this perfect, shining moment, I feel complete. All my dreams have come true, with the woman I adore by my side.

Rising, I scoop her into my arms and carry her to the leather couch. I sit and settle her on my lap, needing to keep her near. She curls into me trustingly, fitting like she was made just for me.

"I hope they have your eyes," I murmur, picturing a little boy or girl with Chrissy's soulful gaze. "And your smile. Your compassion."

"And your strength," she adds softly, tracing my jaw. "Your loyalty and big heart. You're going to be an amazing father, Zander."

Emotion clogs my throat. I swallow hard. "You've already made me a better man, Chrissy. Now you've given me the most incredible gift. I'll spend my life cherishing you both."

I seal my vow with a deep, tender kiss, pouring all my love and devotion into it. She responds with equal fervor, winding her arms around my neck. The kiss turns heated, desire simmering in my veins. I trail my lips down her neck, suckling the sensitive spot behind her ear.

"Let me show you how grateful I am, Mrs. Shaw," I rasp, hands molding her curves. "Let me worship this gorgeous body growing my child."

She shivers, melting into my touch. "Please, Zander. I need you."

I take my time undressing her, layering each new expanse of skin with ardent kisses and caresses. She's a goddess, my very own fertility queen, ripe and lush. I lay her bare before me, a feast for my eyes and hands and mouth.

I make love to her slowly, reverently, savoring each breathy moan and sigh of bliss. I bring her to the peak again and again, wringing out her pleasure until she's boneless and sated beneath me. Only then do I allow my own release, spilling deep inside her, a benediction.

After, I gather her close, nuzzling her damp temple. My perfect wife.

Want a free book from Emma Bray? Go to www.authoremmabray.com.

Keep reading for an excerpt from Unmasking the Billionaire.

Eve

"I can't believe I let you talk me into this!" I

practically have to yell over the music to be heard by Jenny, my best friend since childhood.

Jenny just smiles her dazzling, millionaire-dollar, rich girl smile at me from behind her sparkling, Swarovski-crystal mask.

We're at some sort of masquerade ball for New York's elite. It's the Halloween party of the season and surprisingly not as stuffy as I'd expected it to be.

Honestly, it's kind of cool with the dim lighting, high-end decorations, elaborate costumes, and all the masked faces on parade, but still.

This isn't my element.

"Oh, come on, Eve! This is fun! You need to lighten up and live a little for once!"

That's easy for her to say. She's a trust fund baby without a care in the world. Her mommy and daddy pay for everything, from her expensive haircut to the designer shoes on her feet. She doesn't have to worry about anything.

Not that I begrudge my bestie anything. I'm glad she hasn't had the same struggles in life I've had. It's how she's able to have that beautiful, happy glow about her.

She doesn't know the worry that I do of how she's going to pay next month's rent or how she's going to juggle the electric bill so that the power doesn't get cut off.

And while she's offered to pay my bills before or let me move in with her, I have way too much pride to accept her offers.

I've been making it on my own since I turned eighteen and aged out of the group home, and I'm not about to start accepting charity now that I'm twenty.

"Your birthday only comes around once a year!" she reminds me, flinging an arm around my shoulder familiarly. "It's time to turn up and party!" She pronounces "party" like "par-tay," and I can't help the smile that ghosts across my lips at her giddiness.

Jenny is a blonde bombshell. Model thin, tan, and tall, she's all bubbly and light whereas I almost look like a goth chick with my midnight black hair, pale complexion, and short stature. And although Jenny's slender, she has a little bit of curves in all the right places.

Me? Nothing. I'm so thin my breasts and ass are laughable at best, and it's not because I don't eat because trust me. I've gone hungry before, and you'll never see me turn down a meal or feign a weak appetite. I can put it away like a football player, and I'm not even the least bit ashamed of it.

At barely five foot, though, I'm teeny tiny and still look like a pre-teen—no matter how much I eat.

My best friend and I are total opposites. She's outgoing whereas I'm quieter. I'm not exactly shy, but I don't have a desire to be the life of the party either. She's like the light, and I'm the dark. Seriously, I was born on All Hallow's Eve, and she was born on Jesus' birthday, a perfect little Christmas baby.

"Come on," Jenny grabs my hand and starts dragging me along with her, "let's go find some hot guys."

I roll my eyes. That's another difference between us. Jenny is boy crazy, and I couldn't care less about the opposite sex. I'm not a lesbian or anything, but I just don't have any experience with men.

Survival has kept me from getting into any serious relationships. The most I've ever done is let a few boyfriends in high school kiss me, and I wasn't impressed with those slobbery attempts, so I've never been tempted to even try anything more.

So, yeah, I'm a twenty-year-old virgin. Pathetic, right?

Jenny drags me by a table filled with Halloween-themed cookies, cakes, and other confections, and my mouth begins to water.

I pull back on her hand to try to stay her. "Let's get some refreshments instead!" I yell to her over the pumping music.

She looks over her shoulder at me and rolls her eyes. "I swear, Eve, you're always freaking hungry. I don't know where you put it all."

I smirk at the obvious envy in her tone. Jenny is the stereotypical gym bunny, counting every calorie she eats to maintain her perfect physique.

"Don't hate," I grin at her smugly before reaching out to grab a miniature black cupcake covered with purple frosting.

I barely have time to pop the bite-sized confection in my mouth before Jenny is yanking on my hand again, pulling me through the crowd.

"Jenny, slow down!" I hiss at her, afraid I'm going to break my neck in these five-inch heels she insisted I wear tonight to make me not look like so much of a smurf. Her words—not mine. Plus, she claims they're just the perfect addition to the lacy black dress she dressed me up in.

I swear sometimes I think Jenny is my friend just because she wants a real-life doll to play dress up with. There's no greater joy for her than dressing me up in fancy clothes, doing my hair and makeup, and dragging me to shit like this with her.

And I go along with it because I love my best friend and want to make her happy.

Her eyes are scanning through all the masculine choices, and then she suddenly stops dead in her tracks.

"Oh. My. God." she breaths out.

"What?" my brows furrow at her melodramatic reaction.

"Check out Mr. Big and Scary," she breathes, and my eyes follow her line of sight and widen when they meet the object of her gaze.

A huge man in a black mask stands in a corner looking surly and brooding, towering over the other guests. The mask covers most of his face except his mouth. Think of the Don Juan mask Gerard Butler wore in *The Point of No Return* scene in that film adaptation of *The Phantom of the Opera*. That's what his mask reminds me of.

His hair is dark brown. It's stylishly disheveled, like it's windblown and wild without looking messy. When he tilts his tumbler up and takes a sip of some liquid that's probably brandy or cognac or something else equally expensive, I watch his suit rustle as his muscles bunch with his movements like it's all the fabric can do to contain the beast within.

I don't know who the hell the guy is or what he

does, but he exudes power and wealth. He's not wearing a costume like the other partygoers. No, he's wearing what I already know is a custom-tailored suit.

I don't need to be able to see all his features to see that he's gorgeous and dark and dangerous-looking. I've never seen a more perfect specimen of male masculinity, and my heart speeds up as my breath catches in my throat.

I've never reacted to a man this way before, and Jenny notices it if the sly, mischievous grin she gives me is any indication.

"I dare you to go over there and kiss him," she elbows me.

I laugh and push her back. "You're crazy! I'm not going to do that! I don't even know the guy."

"Exactly!" Jenny's eyes are excited. "You don't know him..." her voice sing-songs, "he's super smexy."

I roll my eyes. Only Jenny would make "smexy" a word in conversation.

Jenny ignores me and goes on, "You're twenty years old today, and you've never had a decent kiss."

I glare at her, suddenly wishing I hadn't told her all the embarrassing details of my failed boyfriends.

Again she ignores me and keeps ticking off reasons I should follow her insane suggestion. "It's dark in here, and you'll never have to see him again. You can simply go lay one on the hot stranger and have a great memory for your birthday, and then we'll go eat cake and dance and party and everything will be perfect! You have nothing to lose and everything to gain!" she says happily.

I stare at her like she's sprouted another head.

Jenny is seriously out of her mind sometimes.

I'm laughing and shaking my head 'no' at her when she narrows her eyes and adds, "Plus, I'll give you a thousand dollars if you do it."

My laugh dies off as I nearly choke. "Whoa, wait. What?" I shake my head at her. "You can't be serious, right?"

Jenny's not laughing, though. She's looking at me challengingly with that I-want-to-get-you-in-trouble look that only a best friend can have.

"Dead serious. I'll give you a thousand bucks to walk over there and kiss that guy." She nods her head in his direction before that evil twinkle enters her eyes again. "And not just a quick peck on the lips. A real kiss. Like with some tongue."

I glance back over at Mr. Smexy. Jesus, did I just refer to him as Mr. Smexy in my head? I obviously need new friends. Jenny is rubbing off on me too much.

The man might be good-looking, but he's terrifying too. God, he could crush me with one hand.

And what the fuck will he think when some random girl comes up and kisses him out of the blue?

He'll probably have me arrested.

I'll embarrass the hell out of myself.

God, am I really considering this?

But, fuck, a thousand dollars? That'd give me a huge boost on paying my bills.

I look back over at Jenny. She's grinning at me impishly. She knows my struggle, and I think she halfway expects me to chicken out and not do it.

And that is what cements my decision.

I cross my arms and tell Jenny, "I want it in cash."

I see the surprise skitter across Jenny's face before she raises one delicate eyebrow and smiles like the Cheshire Cat, the glee practically oozing off her as she claps her hands together and laughs, "You got it, babe."

Before I lose my nerve, I take a deep breath, square my shoulders, and begin making my way over to the corner where Mr. Smexy skulks like some kind of standoffish canine.

I can almost feel Jenny's eyes boring a hole into my back, taking in the whole scene.

A thousand dollars. A thousand dollars, I chant in my head with each step I take.

As I get closer to him, he starts to notice my approach.

His head tips up, and his eyes laser in on me. The lighting is so dim where he's standing, it's hard to make out his features, but his eyes are golden and almost seem to glow like he's a vampire or wolf or something.

I swallow nervously and try to calm my racing heart.

A thousand dollars. A thousand dollars.

I just hope he doesn't bite me.

———

Lucian

My eyes are trained on a tiny form making its way in my direction, and they narrow as it gets closer.

It's dark in here, and lights flash out on the dance floor, but I've sequestered myself in this corner for a reason.

I don't want to be bothered.

In fact, the only reason I'm here is to meet with a business associate, and the fucker is late.

I'd much rather be back at my mansion. Alone. Secluded. The way I like to be.

I have no use for people beyond employing them.

Social settings aren't my scene and for good reason. The only reason I agreed to see my associate here is because he's only going to be in town for one night, and this is where he's going to be.

For some God forsaken reason.

And it's a masquerade-themed Halloween ball, so I can cover my scarred face. It's not that I particularly give a fuck what people think about it. I know that I'm still considered handsome, that maybe the cut that spans right side of my visage simply gives me that allure of danger that some women find so enticing.

But it's the questions I can't stand. The curiosity. The goddamned nosiness.

People don't know me. Nobody seeks me out. My demeanor is just menacing enough to off-put any curious eyes that glance my way.

So why in the hell does this little slip of a thing seem to be walking my way?

My eyes take in her long, dark tresses that flow

down to her impossibly tiny waist. Milky white skin that almost seems to glow in the darkness.

Fuck, she's covered in lace. Her dress must be corseted if the way the two little globes of her breasts are pushed up is any indication. They're not large by any means, but just the sight of that little bit of modest cleavage has my blood roaring in my veins.

How long has it been since I've been with a woman? Since before the incident five years ago at least. I know I have enough money that I can still have plenty of women on my arm if I want.

That's not what I want, though. Shallow companions, fake smiles.

Since I can't have a connection, something real, I settle for nothing.

My hands work just fine.

But Christ Almighty, seeing a female approaching me after all this time has every nerve in my body pulled taut. I'm on edge and feel like I could blow at any moment.

My eyes drag back up her form to her head, most of which is covered with an elaborate peacock mask.

I can't make out her features through the dim lighting and all the ostentatious feathers that cover her face, but I see a flash of midnight blue before she's suddenly standing right in front of me. Her body isn't touching mine, but she's so close that I can feel her heat through our clothes, smell her scent. Violets and vanilla and something I can't identify.

Her head barely reaches my chest, and before I can ask her what she's doing, who she is, hell, anything, I hear her take a deep breath, and then she clumsily grabs my face and pulls it down to hers, pressing her lips firmly, if somewhat nervously, against mine.

I'm so stunned I don't react at first. But then my mind and body registers the feel of her tiny lips on mine. They're pressing softly against them, and then she takes my bottom lip in between her lips in an innocent, single-lip kiss. It's unpracticed, but god there's something so fucking hot about it, I feel a drop of precum bead the tip of my suddenly hard cock.

Hunger, hot and immediate, roars in my chest and bleeds through my veins.

I don't think. I just react, my hand reaching out to fist in her hair as I angle her head up to mine, deepening the kiss.

I suck on her bottom lip before my tongue forces her mouth to part, and she does so with a gasp of surprise.

I lick inside her mouth and taste her. Fucking hell, she tastes so goddamned sweet. Like pure sugar.

She whimpers, and that sound only spurs me on. I growl and mate my tongue with hers, desperate for more. More of her mouth. More of her.

I don't know who the fuck she is, but I know I'm not just turned into an animal because of five years of abstinence.

This is something more. Something primal. Like a wolf imprinting on its mate.

She tastes so fucking *right*. That might be a cliche, but fuck if I can help what I'm thinking and feeling.

Never, I mean, *never*, has a mere kiss affected me this way.

Just as I manage to set my glass of cognac down on a nearby table and am getting ready to pull her flush against my body, maybe throw her over my shoulder and stomp out of here caveman style and take her back to my lair and make her mine, she pulls away harshly, her little hands pressing hard against my chest.

We're both panting. I watch her little chest moving up and down as she gasps for breath. Her lips are ruby red and puffy and swollen from our kiss. I'm dying to see her eyes again, to demand who she is, where she came from, why the hell she planted her little lips on mine, but I never get a chance to ask any of that because she never looks back up at me.

Quick as a flash, she turns and runs away from me.

Panic explodes in my chest when I see her flying through the crowd.

Just as I start to take off after her, Adrian shows up and claps a heavy hand on my shoulder.

"Lucian, my man!" he greets me jovially.

I glance over at him distractedly, irritated that he took my attention off my little raven.

By the time I look back into the crowd, she's nowhere to be found. Rage and loss bubble up inside me to create a nauseating cocktail of emotions.

And I want to fucking murder someone.

Get Unmasking the Billionaire here: Unmasking the Billionaire.